I SURVIVED

THE BLACK DEATH, 1348

by Lauren Tarshis

illustrated by Scott Dawson

Scholastic Inc.

Text copyright © 2024 by Dreyfuss Tarshis Media Inc.
Illustrations copyright © 2024 by Scholastic Inc.

Photos ©: 117 top left: The Print Collector/Print Collector/Getty Images; 117 top right: Science History Images/Alamy Stock Photo; 117 bottom: Fine Art Images/Heritage Images/Getty Images; 119: Zuri Swimmer/Alamy Stock Photo; 120: Pictorial Press Ltd/Alamy Stock Photo; 122: Jim West/Alamy Stock Photo; 123: Rapp Halour/Alamy Stock Photo; 127: Alex Hannam/Alamy Stock Photo; 128: BarksJapan/Alamy Stock Photo; 129: Quagga Media/Alamy Stock Photo; 131: Universal History Archive/Universal Images Group/Getty Images; 133: Library of Congress/Corbis/VCG via Getty Images; 134: HISTORY, CULTURE/Alamy Stock Photo; 135: CDC/Christina Nelson, MD/Science Source.

Special thanks to Benjamin Dodds

ISBN 978-1-338-89180-5

10 9 8 7 6 5 4 3 2 1   24 25 26 27 28

Printed in the U.S.A.   40
First printing 2024
Designed by Katie Fitch

For Valerie

CHAPTER 1

I'm dying.

That's all eleven-year-old Elsie Archer was thinking as she lay on a sweat-soaked straw mattress. Burning with fever, head throbbing, Elsie thrashed and moaned. The air around her stunk of sickness . . . and death.

What was happening? Was she locked in a rat-filled dungeon? Was she trapped in a burning castle? Had she been snatched from her bed by a fire-breathing dragon?

The answer was more terrifying than any

nightmare. Elsie had been struck by one of the deadliest diseases in the history of the world — a plague that became known as the Black Death. Already it had killed millions — in China and India, in cities all around the Black Sea. From there it spread to Italy and France. And now it was sweeping across England, where Elsie lived.

The disease was likely spread by infected fleas. They'd bite into the flesh of rats and suck their blood. When the rats died, the fleas would feed on humans instead.

But this was not known in the 1300s, when Elsie lived. Even the smartest people didn't understand why people got sick. Was it some kind of curse? A punishment from the heavens? Had an earthquake leaked poisonous air from deep underground?

Elsie was living in a time before vaccines, before doctors knew about germs. All she knew for sure was that something terrible was happening. Lying in the darkness, she felt like an evil creature was living inside her body. It was chewing on her bones, crushing her lungs, pounding on her skull.

She cried out for Papa; her Granny; for her best friend, Humphrey. Were they sick, too?

But she could barely speak. Or breathe.

It seemed impossible that she would come through this alive.

And if she did, she had no idea what in her world — or who — would be left.

CHAPTER 2

"Aaaaaaaaaaa-CHHHHHOOOOOOO!"

Humphrey's sneeze blasted through the forest.

"God bless you," Elsie said.

Saying *God bless you* chased away evil spirits. They were always trying to sneak into your brain through your nose. Everyone knew that.

4

"Thank you," Humphrey said.

"I think you are the loudest sneezer in England," Elsie said. "King Edward himself might have heard you all the way in London."

"Good morning, Your Majesty!" Humphrey shouted, wiping his freckled nose on the sleeve of his rough wool tunic.

Elsie laughed. "You're such a fopdoodle," she said, giving her best friend a little shove.

It was a chilly fall morning and Elsie and Humphrey were walking through the thick, dark forest at the edge of their village. They were hunting for a rabbit. Elsie wanted to surprise her grandmother with meat for rabbit stew.

Granny was mad at her — again. And not for the usual reasons, like Elsie ignoring her chores or falling asleep in church or stomping into the house with mud-caked boots. Granny was mad because Elsie had shot an arrow at a rich kid named Perkin. Elsie hadn't hurt him. She'd aimed perfectly, so the arrow shot the fancy hat right off Perkin's thick skull.

And he deserved it! Perkin was a bully. He

was always tripping someone into a puddle or making some little kid cry. Even Granny knew he was a rotten goose egg. Someone had to teach him a lesson!

But Perkin's father didn't see it that way. After church he'd cornered Granny.

"The girl is wild!" he'd shouted. "She needs to be locked up. A few weeks in a dungeon will teach her how to behave!"

Would Granny really send her to a dungeon? Elsie didn't think so. But Elsie still needed to make it up to Granny. Hopefully some juicy rabbit meat would do the trick. Elsie just had to make sure Granny didn't find out she and Humphrey had come all the way to the forest to find a rabbit. Kids weren't allowed here on their own. Wolves lived here. Kidnappers and outlaws, too. Who knew what other dangers lurked in the shadows of these tall, twisting trees?

But Elsie wasn't scared. She and Humphrey were too bony for a wolf's breakfast. Kidnappers wouldn't waste time on them, either. They went after the children of rich people who lived in castles and rode around in shiny carriages. They wouldn't bother with raggedy peasant kids in patched clothes.

As for outlaws, Elsie was keeping her eyes open. A few weeks back, their small village church had been robbed. The thieves had gotten away with the church's only precious treasure — a silver bowl, ringed with small rubies. It was used for holy water. Everyone in the village was sure it was stolen by outlaws lurking somewhere in these woods.

Elsie gripped the bow Papa had given her for her eighth birthday. Four freshly made arrows were strapped to her back. She'd come here to shoot a rabbit. But one of her arrows would work just as well on a vile outlaw.

"Elsie!" Humphrey cried. "A baby dragon!" He pointed to a little green lizard that was sunning itself on a rock near the stream.

Elsie grinned at Humphrey's joke. When they were little, they were sure dragons were real. Giants and magic, too. Papa was always telling them stories.

"Long ago and far away," he'd begin.

Their favorite story was about a ferocious dragon that terrorized the land. The beast was taller than a castle tower, with red glowing eyes and a stinging tail. Its scorching breath could set fire to a forest in one puff. It fed on children, plucking them from their beds with its massive claws.

Screee screee screee! it would shriek as it swooped down from the sky.

Elsie and Humphrey would shiver in fear! And of course, they wanted to hear the story over and over. The best part was the end, when the brave knight conquered the dragon!

Humphrey faced the lizard. He snatched a stick from the ground and held it out like it was a shiny blade.

"Back, you wicked beast!" he shouted.

The lizard stared at Humphrey with its big, sleepy eyes. It flicked its tongue.

"Come and get me," it seemed to say.

Humphrey let out another one of his thunder sneezes.

"Aaaaaaaaaaaa-CHHHHHOOOOOOO!"

The lizard skittered away.

"You did it, Humphrey!" Elsie laughed.

"Aaaaaaaaaaaa-CHHHHHOOOOOOO!"

"Aaaaaaaaaaaa-CHHHHHOOOOOOO!"

"Aaaaaaaaaaaa-CHHHHHOOOOOOO!"

Yikes!

Humphrey turned to Elsie. His eyes were filled with fear.

"What's wrong?" Elsie said, glancing around, half wondering if there really was a dragon — or a wolf — about to attack them.

"Elsie," he said quietly, dropping his fake sword. "What if I have it?"

"Have what?" Elsie asked.

"The plague!"

CHAPTER 3

The plague?

Elsie stared at Humphrey. What was he talking about?

And then she remembered — a new kind of sickness. They'd heard about it a few weeks ago, from a traveler.

Everyone in the village got excited when a traveler came through sleepy little Brambly. Travelers brought important news, like the marriage of Princess Joan.

The king's fourteen-year-old daughter was

going to marry a Spanish prince. Just last month she'd sailed off to Spain. People in Brambly were still talking about the princess. Last week at market day, the blacksmith's little daughters had been skipping around wearing flower crowns.

"We're Princess Joan!" they sang.

Elsie looked at Humphrey now, remembering how he'd bowed to them, flashing his goofy smile. The girls had burst into giggles.

But nobody was singing or giggling when this latest traveler shared his plague story.

He'd stood in the middle of the village square on market day.

"People of Brambly!" he'd boomed. "You are all in terrible danger!"

People had gathered around him, including Elsie and Humphrey. They loved market day. Granny sometimes gave them a coin so they could buy a sweet cake to share.

The traveling man had looked at the crowd with wild, raving eyes.

"There's a deadly sickness sweeping the world,"

he'd said. "A plague. It brings on a terrible fever, agonizing thirst, and bone-crushing pains."

But the worst part, he said, were huge lumps that erupted under the arms and thighs.

"They're called buboes," he said. "They swell up with blood and pus, and then they explode."

The whole crowd had seemed to groan at once. Elsie almost puked up her sweet cake.

"There's no stopping this plague," the man went on.

Already it had spread from country to country. It had crossed mountains and oceans. Millions were dead.

"And now, good people," the man said, "this illness is coming to England. Soon it will be here, in your quiet village. It's coming for you!"

He'd scared everyone half to death!

"But now I have happy news for you all," he said, opening a sack hanging from his belt. "I can protect you from this plague with one of my magical charms!"

He pulled out what looked to everyone like a plain old black river stone.

"Buy one of my charms for just two coins, and you will be forever protected from this dreaded illness!"

That's when everyone realized he was a liar! There was no new sickness, no deadly plague. The man just wanted to scare people into buying his worthless charms! What a crook!

"Shame on him!" Granny had said.

An angry mob had chased the man out of town.

Elsie had forgotten all about that lying man and his fake sickness.

But his story must have seeped into Humphrey's brain, like a sneaky evil spirit.

"I have been feeling hot," he said now, resting his hand on his forehead. He smacked his lips. "And thirsty."

He started groping around his shoulder and in his armpit.

"Oh no . . . ," he groaned.

"What?" Elsie asked.

"I have a bubo!"

"A what?" Elsie asked.

"A bubo! A plague lump!"

Elsie cringed.

"I'm dead!" Humphrey cried.

"Let me see," Elsie said, suddenly nervous.

Humphrey rolled up the floppy sleeve of his tunic and lifted his arm.

Elsie gasped, leaping back in horror.

CHAPTER 4

"Humphrey!" Elsie rasped. "You stink!" She flapped her hand in front of her nose. "When was the last time you took a bath?"

He smelled like he had a dead mouse living under his arm!

Humphrey frowned.

"A bath?" he asked. "I don't know . . . a few months ago? Baths are dangerous!"

That was true, Elsie knew. "But you still need to wash," she said.

Elsie pinched her nose and peered under Humphrey's arm.

"There's no . . . *bubo*," she said. "There's just a little mosquito bite. You've been scratching it for days."

She put her hand on his forehead. "And you don't have a fever. You're as cool as an apple."

"What about my sneezing?" Humphrey asked.

"You just have the snivels — like I had last week. Remember how I was sneezing? Granny made me drink that broth that tasted like old feet!"

She'd also made Elsie a special mint tea with honey and her favorite soup. Granny was the town healer. She wasn't a doctor — only men could do that. Most doctors in England were monks or priests. But there wasn't a church hospital near Brambly. So, when someone was sick, Granny tended to them. She also helped deliver babies.

"There is no such thing as the plague," Elsie said to Humphrey. "That man was a crook, remember?"

"You're right," Humphrey said, taking a deep breath.

Relieved, Elsie led the way up a muddy hill and along a deer path. A fallen oak tree with a trunk as wide as a barrel blocked their way, so they climbed over it. Hopefully Humphrey would forget about this made-up sickness. Because Elsie had enough to worry about.

It wasn't Granny being mad — Elsie knew Granny loved her, no matter what. Her big worry was Papa. He'd been gone for more than two years fighting in the war against the French. He was a special kind of soldier. Not a knight in armor who fought with a sword and lance. Mostly it was the sons of rich and important people who could become knights.

Papa was a longbowman — a kind of archer. The longbow was huge — taller and heavier than Elsie. It took great strength to pull back the string. But a longbow shot arrows farther and faster than any other kind of bow. And the arrows were tipped with steel, strong enough to stab through a knight's armor.

In a big battle, thousands of archers lined up to face the enemy knights.

Their commander shouted out the special archer orders.

Make ready your bows!

Nock!

Aim!

Loose!

Thousands of arrows would fill the sky. They'd pour down like stabbing raindrops. The archers would fire again, again, and again, four arrows a minute.

Feshoom! Feshoom! Feshoom! Feshoom!

Elsie hadn't seen or heard from Papa in two years. They couldn't write letters to each other — neither of them could write or read. Hardly anyone in their village could.

All she and Granny knew about Papa was bits of news travelers shared. He was alive, they'd heard not long ago. And so far, the English were winning the war.

If only Elsie could be with Papa right now, fighting the French alongside him. But girls weren't allowed to become longbowmen. Or priests or doctors or blacksmiths or cobblers . . . or much of anything.

Elsie kicked a stone out of their path.

It wasn't right!

How many times had she said those words to herself?

She eyed Humphrey as they pushed their way through a tangle of branches. Was it right that he'd lost both his parents by the time he was five? He now lived with his sour-faced Uncle Ralph. Elsie's mother was gone, too — she'd passed away right after Elsie was born.

And what about Lord Norling? He was the nobleman who owned Brambly, this forest, and all villages and towns for miles around. He lived in a castle, feasting on roasted peacock and spiced meats. Meanwhile, most people around here were peasants, earning a penny a day for their labor. Their two-room houses were made of mud and tree branches.

That wasn't right at all!

Yes, Elsie was better off than most. Papa's

archer salary was five coins a month, far more than most peasants earned. Their house had three whole rooms. Elsie even wore a dress that was blue — a color only rich people could afford. Granny had gotten the blue fabric as a thank-you present from the town's wool seller. She'd saved his son's life after he'd fallen through the river ice.

Elsie looked down at her blue dress. It was beautiful, even though it was patched and faded by now. But even ten blue dresses couldn't make up for all that was wrong.

If only . . .

"Elsie!"

Humphrey's voice jolted Elsie out of her faraway thoughts. He was pointing to a plump brown rabbit.

Elsie snatched an arrow from her quiver and loaded it in her little bow.

"Come on!" Elsie said.

The rabbit led them on a zigzag chase, deeper and deeper into the forest. They wound up in a thicket of trees. But before they could catch it, sounds echoed from somewhere close.

The *clop-clop-clop* of horse hooves. The jangle of stirrups. Men's voices — shouting, cursing, rough laughter.

Outlaws!

CHAPTER 5

Outlaws were snake-hearted criminals who spent their lives on the run. They robbed travelers on the road. They broke into rich people's houses and grabbed bags of coins and jewels. They stole cows and horses and goats from poor peasants. They killed people without a thought.

The men's voices were getting louder — they were coming this way! Elsie swung her head around, looking for a way out. But tall pricker bushes blocked their path forward. There was no way to escape in time.

They scurried behind a thick bush and crouched down. Seconds later the men appeared. Elsie counted seven of them.

Her heart pounded as she studied them through the leaves — their tangled beards and wild hair, their rumpled cloaks. Leggings and boots caked with mud.

Their filthy clothes were brightly colored, made of velvet and fine wool, decorated with golden threads, silver buttons, and buckles. Elsie tried not to think about what had happened to the rich people who'd worn those clothes first.

But wait . . . One of the men looked different from the rest. He was tall, with small black eyes and a neatly clipped beard. His black tunic and leggings were clean, his boots shiny. A finely made sword hung from his belt.

"It's Sheriff Grimwood!" Elsie whispered to Humphrey.

He worked for the king.

He was a brutal man — everyone in Brambly hated him. Still, with the sheriff here, Elsie and

Humphrey wouldn't be kidnapped by the outlaws.

But then her skin prickled. What was Grimwood doing with a band of outlaws? He wasn't arresting them. He was laughing and swearing along with them. As if they were friends.

Or maybe he was just pretending to be friends with them, so he could lure them into a trap? No matter what was happening, Elsie and Humphrey needed to stay dead quiet. Elsie prayed the outlaws passed quickly.

But about ten footsteps away, the men stopped their horses.

"This is the place," barked the outlaw leading the way. He was a dangerous-looking man with a barrel chest and massive arms. His beard was clumped with dirt and shiny with grease.

"Let's see what you have for me," Grimwood said.

Have for him?

Something very strange was happening here, Elsie was sure.

The men all got off their horses. Two of the outlaws tramped into the bushes. Moments later they came out hauling a large wooden chest. They dropped it in front of the sheriff.

Dirty Beard lifted the lid.

Grimwood pulled out a silver bowl. Elsie's mouth fell open in shock. Humphrey gasped.

It was the stolen bowl from their church!

Grimwood reached into the chest again, inspecting shiny golden cups, jeweled candlesticks, bowls glittering with gems.

"Very good," he said, closing the lid. "I'll be back in a few days with some of my men. We'll bring everything to London to sell. Don't worry. You'll get your share."

And that's when it hit Elsie, like a kick in the gut.

Grimwood wasn't tricking these outlaws. He was working with them!

Elsie couldn't believe it.

Grimwood was known for being very strict. He brutally punished anyone who broke the law. His hangings and whippings and tortures weren't

only for violent criminals. A person could get their hand chopped off for stealing a loaf of bread.

Elsie's eyes narrowed with fury. He was worse than an outlaw! He was supposed to be protecting people!

Grimwood dropped the precious treasures back in the chest.

The two outlaws returned the chest to its hiding place. The men got back onto their horses. They looked just about ready to move when Humphrey grabbed Elsie's arm.

"*Aaaaaah . . . ahhhhh . . .*"

Oh no! He was going to sneeze!

Humphrey's face twisted. His cheeks turned bright red as he tried to hold in the sneeze. But there was no stopping it.

"*Aaaaaaa —*"

CHAPTER 6

Elsie turned and grabbed Humphrey into a crushing hug, so that his face was pressed tight against her shoulder.

She managed to muffle the sound.

Ahhhh-pffffffff!

The sound was loud. But it didn't sound much like a sneeze.

"What was that?" Grimwood asked, stopping his horse. The other men stopped, too.

They all looked around.

Elsie and Humphrey huddled closer and

crouched down, making themselves as small as they could. Elsie's guts squirmed like eels in a barrel. She tried not to think about those outlaws' daggers stabbing into her.

Elsie put an arm around Humphrey and took deep breaths.

Time seemed to stop.

"Sounded like a sick duck," Dirty Beard said finally. "Let's move."

Elsie and Humphrey waited until the voices faded away. They crept out of their hiding place.

Elsie was shaking and Humphrey looked like he might faint. Elsie looked over toward the bushes where the treasure chest was hidden. Now was their chance to get their church treasure back. That's what Papa would do!

But she was too scared. She just wanted to get out of this forest. Her heart pounded as they crept carefully along, steering clear of the main deer path the men would have taken.

Every sound — a rustle of leaves, a cracking twig — stopped them short. They held their breath, clutching hands, looking around with wide eyes filled with fear.

But they saw no sign of Grimwood or the outlaws.

At last, they stepped out of the forest gloom. Elsie looked up and saw their church steeple in the distance. She almost cried with relief.

"We're safe," Humphrey said.

They ran into a meadow and collapsed.

"We have to tell people what we saw," Elsie said breathlessly.

Humphrey shook his head.

"We can't," Humphrey said. "Then everyone will know we were in the forest."

Everyone — including Granny. She'd be furious!

"But we can't let him get away with this!" Elsie said, yanking up a handful of grass and throwing it. "And we need to get the church treasure back before they sell it in London."

Humphrey scrunched his eyebrows together — his thinking face.

"What about Jonah?" Humphrey said.

Jonah was Papa's best friend, like an uncle to Elsie and Humphrey. Years ago, Jonah and Papa had fought together in the Scottish wars.

"He just got back from a trip," Humphrey added.

Jonah was a kind of deliveryman. He rode his horse wagon back and forth between the towns around Brambly and the big cities along England's coast. This latest trip was to a city called Melcombe. It had a port where big sailing ships arrived with fine fabric and wines and spices from faraway lands.

Elsie smiled at Humphrey — Jonah was the perfect person to talk to about Grimwood. He always had good ideas. And he wouldn't tell Granny they'd been in the forest.

They went straight to Jonah's small house, which was at the edge of the village. His trusty horse, Kibby, was grazing in the field. He looked up and greeted them with a snort.

Jonah's wagon was standing near the door. Elsie glimpsed into the wagon. It was piled high with bright red wool fabric he must have picked up in Melcombe. Something seemed to be wriggling around under the fabric. Elsie smiled to herself — Jonah's white cat, Willow, loved to play hide-and-seek.

"I know it's you," Elsie said, pulling back the fabric.

But it wasn't Willow. It was a rat! It was huge and black with glinting eyes.

And before Elsie could take a step back, the creature leapt up, jaws open, its teeth aimed at Elsie's throat.

CHAPTER 7

Elsie stumbled back and let out a loud shriek. The rat just missed her, landing with a thud in front of her muddy boots.

It hissed at Elsie and skittered away.

Elsie shuddered.

The front door swung open and a small, muscular man with red hair and a matching beard came out.

Jonah.

"What's happened?" he said with alarm.

"A rat attacked Elsie!" Humphrey said.

"It didn't attack me," Elsie said. "I was just . . . startled."

What a fool she was, shrieking over a little rat!

Willow the cat came out the door, padding over to see what the fuss was about. Elsie reached down and picked her up, rubbing her cheek against her soft fur.

"I've never seen a black rat like that," Humphrey said.

"I bet it came from France," Jonah said. "They hide on the ships, then get off when the ships dock in England. One of them must have snuck onto my wagon when I was loading the fabric. I think it wanted to see my fancy house."

He smirked as he glanced at his little house with the drooping roof.

They all laughed. Willow purred.

Elsie put the cat down. If it was a normal day, she and Humphrey would plop down at Jonah's table. He always came back with stories from sailors and traders. Like the one about a smiling fish that danced on its tail — a dolphin. And a fruit that looked like a hairy brown rock — a coconut. Crack it open, and sweet milk poured out.

Elsie loved hearing these stories, even if she wasn't totally sure they were true.

But they hadn't come to Jonah's today to hear stories. Elsie's stomach clenched.

"Jonah," she said, putting Willow down. "Grim . . ."

But Jonah wasn't listening. He'd grabbed a pile of fabric from his wagon.

"Help me get the fabric into the house," he called out. "It's going to rain. Kibby's ears are twitching."

Horses' ears often twitched when bad weather was coming. Everyone knew that.

Elsie and Humphrey each grabbed a pile of fabric and headed inside.

Elsie ran a hand over the fabric. She couldn't believe how soft it was. Before she knew it, she'd wrapped some around herself.

"You look like Princess Joan," Humphrey said with a chuckle.

Elsie cracked a smile. But then she felt itchy pricks on her neck. She dropped the fabric and slapped at her neck. When she brought her hand away, her palm was speckled with dead fleas and smeared with blood.

"The fabric is crawling with fleas!" she exclaimed.

"I know," Jonah said with a shrug, picking up

the fabric and laying it in a big stack in the corner. "I'm covered with bites. But a few fleas never hurt anyone."

Elsie's eyes welled up, and she quickly turned away so Jonah wouldn't see. But of course it wasn't the fleas upsetting her.

"Grimwood is helping outlaws!" she blurted out.

Jonah's face darkened. "Why would you say that?"

"We were in the forest," Humphrey said. "We saw him."

Jonah listened with wide eyes as Elsie and Humphrey told him everything they'd seen in the forest — Grimwood with the outlaws, the chest of loot, their own church bowl.

"Sit," he said sharply, pointing to the table. He brought three mugs and a crock of cider to the table. He said nothing as he filled the mugs, but there was no hiding the worry in his eyes. He drank his cider in one gulp and refilled his mug. He drank that, too.

He took a deep breath.

"Did Grimwood see *you*?" he asked.

"No," Humphrey said.

Jonah exhaled with relief.

"Thank the saints for that. But you need to listen to me very closely." His eyes flicked from Elsie to Humphrey. "You must never tell anyone what you saw today. It will only bring terrible trouble for you and for Brambly."

Elsie's mouth dropped open. Jonah was making no sense!

"But Grimwood is a criminal!" she said. "Everyone needs to know!"

"He should be in jail," Humphrey added.

"And what about the church bowl?" Elsie continued. "We saw it with our own eyes!"

Grimwood couldn't get away with this. It wasn't right!

"Forget about the bowl," Jonah said so sharply that Willow leapt from his lap and bolted into the next room. "Grimwood will destroy anyone who threatens him. Even two young children. He's a monster."

Elsie stared at Jonah. His scared expression chilled her to the bone.

Jonah was a fearless soldier. In Scotland, he'd saved Papa's life from an attacking knight.

What could Grimwood have done to make a person like Jonah so scared?

Jonah seemed to read the question in her mind.

"Has anyone ever told you the story about a village called Westerly?" he asked.

Elsie and Humphrey shook their heads.

"It's time you heard it."

CHAPTER 8

Jonah poured himself another mug of cider and drank it quickly. Elsie had never seen anyone so thirsty.

"Westerly was about seven miles from here," Jonah began. "It was a beautiful place, with a small castle, a beautiful green, and a busy market square. About ten years ago, Grimwood was there with some of his men. They drank ale in the tavern and then decided to race their horses. They galloped right into the village green. It was market day."

Elsie pictured Brambly on market day, packed

with shoppers and farmers and children.

"There were five men on big horses," Jonah went on. "They just plowed right through the crowd. People had to dive to get out of the way."

He rushed his hand across the table as if it were a galloping horse. His mug went flying. Elsie caught it before it tumbled off the table.

"But one girl couldn't get out of Grimwood's path. She fell. Grimwood didn't even try to stop or turn. He mowed her down, like she was a stalk of wheat. She died instantly. She was just twelve years old."

Elsie remembered a man in Brambly who'd been trampled by a runaway horse. Friends put him on a cart and brought him to Elsie's house so Granny could help him. Elsie caught just a glimpse of his broken body. But she'd never forget the sight of white bone jutting through his flesh. His clothes were blood soaked. His face was purple with bruises.

There was nothing Granny — or anyone — could do to help the man.

"Grimwood and his men rode off. The whole town came to the girl's funeral. People wanted Grimwood and the men arrested — hanged."

Jonah sat back. Suddenly he looked very pale, and tired.

"Practically the whole town had seen what Grimwood had done," he went on. "A group planned to go to Lord Norling's castle and demand justice. But Grimwood found out. The night before they were set to go, the town was attacked.

"Ten masked men crept into the town. They were carrying torches. They spread out and set fire to anything that would burn — houses, shops, fields of grain. They climbed the castle walls and attacked the guards. They set fire to everything inside. People from town tried to fight back. But it was the middle of the night and nobody was prepared. Almost everything in the town was destroyed."

"And it was Grimwood?" Elsie asked in shock.

"And everyone knew it," Jonah said, nodding. "But he and his men were all masked. So, there was no real proof. And by then, the people of Westerly were terrified. They'd lost everything. The town had to be abandoned. Today, it no longer exists."

No wonder Elsie had never heard of it.

"So now I hope you understand," Jonah said. "You must put this behind you."

"We will," Humphrey said in a fearful voice.

Jonah stood and rubbed his temples. "All this talk of Grimwood has given me a nasty headache. I'm going to lie down. I'll see you at the market tomorrow."

He opened the door for them.

"Elsie," Jonah said, fixing his gaze on her. "Promise me you are going to forget about Grimwood. You must stay out of the forest."

Elsie managed a nod.

She felt like she'd just lost a bloody battle, even though she'd never fired a shot.

Walking back home with Humphrey, Elsie seethed with fury. Those familiar, bitter words shouted through her mind.

It's not right! It's not right!

She pictured Grimwood's black crow eyes. She imagined that girl's broken body. The castle in flames. She could practically feel the fire scorching her skin.

Grimwood wasn't just a criminal. He was a killer. A fire starter.

He was like the dragon from Papa's tale!

And that silver bowl with the rubies, the treasure their village had cherished for hundreds of years. It was lost forever.

But wait . . . Was it really lost?

It was still in the forest, in that chest. Grimwood had said he wasn't returning to get the loot for a few days.

And that's when the idea came to Elsie, popping into her head so suddenly it slowed her down.

There was nothing stopping her from getting that church treasure back. Yes, she'd be breaking her promise to Jonah. But maybe he'd never have to know.

Humphrey was studying her. "What are you thinking?" he asked.

"I . . ." She swallowed her words. "I'm just thinking about that disgusting rat."

She wasn't going to tell her plan to Humphrey. He'd just try to talk her out of it.

Elsie lifted her chin, suddenly feeling a few inches taller.

Here was her chance to do something.

For once, she could make things right.

CHAPTER 9

THE NEXT MORNING
BRAMBLY VILLAGE GREEN

"What a beautiful day," Granny said as they wove through the market crowd.

They walked past the stalls piled high with fruits and vegetables, barrels of cider and ale, wheels of cheese as big as wagon wheels. The blacksmith's daughters, Abra and Lucy, ran past Elsie wearing their Princess Joan flower crowns.

"Hi, Elsie!" they squealed.

"Hello, princesses!" Elsie called back.

Elsie painted on a jolly smile.

But all she could think about was her plan for later.

As soon as their shopping was finished, Granny was going to visit her friend, the Widow Brewster. She was even older than Granny — forty-seven! Elsie would take their basket home and then go into the forest. She'd find the church bowl, hurry back, and hide it somewhere. Tomorrow morning, before sunrise, she'd sneak into the church and put it back on the altar.

Nobody would ever know how it got there. Let them think an angel had returned it. Even Humphrey wouldn't know. He'd told her he'd be busy today, helping his Uncle Ralph chop wood.

Now she just needed Granny to hurry up. But everywhere they went, Granny stopped to chat.

"Foot feeling better?" she asked Edward the butcher as he cut them a hunk of juicy ham. Not long ago he dropped his knife and nearly cut off his big toe. Granny stitched it back on for him.

"Good as new, thanks to you," he said.

Next, they stopped to buy bread from Robert the baker.

"How's your beautiful baby girl?" Granny asked his cheerful wife, Tilda.

"Getting big!" she said.

Granny had delivered practically every baby here in Brambly. Three were named after her — Gertrude — including Tilda and Robert's little girl.

Their basket got heavier. Elsie got more and more impatient. But people kept stopping Granny to talk. Wanda the egg lady made Granny look at the wart on her chin. Oliver the apple man showed her the long hairs growing out of his ear.

Elsie thought she might jump out of her skin. Her itchy flea bites only made her more jittery.

At last Granny announced they were finished.

"Did you see Jonah?" Granny asked as she tightened her cloak. "He's always at the market."

Elsie shook her head.

Jonah had said he'd be at the market, but he

had seemed so tired from his trip yesterday. It wasn't surprising he had stayed home.

"Why don't you go over to his house and invite him to dinner," Granny said.

Elsie promised she would. She'd have plenty of time after she got back from the forest.

Granny reached into her purse and pulled out a small coin.

"Buy yourself a sweet cake," she said with her warm smile.

She handed the coin to Elsie with a quick peck on the cheek. She smelled like flowers and mint.

"Thank you, Granny," Elsie said.

She felt a pang of guilt.

Granny did so much for her — for everyone in the village. Elsie needed to help her more and follow the rules.

And she would.

Starting tomorrow.

CHAPTER 10

Elsie lugged the heavy basket across the village green. That's when she noticed Abra and Lucy. They were huddled together, crying. An older boy stood next to them, dressed in a bright purple tunic with a sparkling silver-buckled belt. Elsie curled her lip into a scowl. Perkin.

What was that nasty snake doing now?

Elsie had sworn to Granny that she'd steer clear of him. But now she put down her basket and raced over to the little girls.

Their faces were streaked with tears. Their flower crowns were in the grass.

Perkin smirked at Elsie, but she ignored him.

"What happened?" Elsie asked the girls, dropping to her knees.

"Perkin said Princess Joan is dead!" Abra cried.

"He said we're all going to die!" said Lucy.

Elsie put her arms around them and glared at Perkin.

"What's wrong with you?" she snapped.

"I was just telling them the truth," Perkin said. "The princess *is* dead. Of the plague. It's coming here, too."

"You're a fool," Elsie said, pulling the girls closer. "Stop spouting lies."

"I'm not lying," he said. "The princess died in France. Her ships stopped there on the way to Spain. The plague is everywhere in France. In Italy and Spain, too. I heard bodies are rotting in the streets. And now it's in England as well. Sick sailors brought it here."

Elsie hugged the girls tighter so they couldn't hear.

"Go away, Perkin!" Elsie hissed.

"I *am* going away. My whole family is leaving

Brambly. Today. We're going to our country house. We'll be long gone when the plague comes. But you'll all be stuck here."

"Liar," Elsie spat.

"You'll see," Perkin said with a nasty glare. "You'll all see."

And then he turned and walked slowly toward his house. Like the few other wealthy people in Brambly, Perkin lived in one of the stone houses close to the green. Elsie had never been inside. But she'd heard there were five whole rooms. The floors were covered with wood, not dirt and dried grass like most others. Too bad being rich didn't make a person nicer!

Elsie dried the girls' tears with her cloak.

"There," she said. "You're both braver than any princess."

She picked up their flower crowns and put them back on their curly heads.

"And don't listen to Perkin," she said. "He's a slimy toad with a rotten goose egg for a head!"

That made them giggle.

Perkin was more than just a bully, Elsie

realized. He enjoyed scaring people, just like Grimwood.

Too bad Elsie didn't have her bow and arrows with her. This time she'd shoot his hat right to the moon!

She reached into the basket and fished out the coin Granny had given her and handed it to Abra.

"Go get yourselves some sweet cakes."

Abra and Lucy gasped. "Thank you, Elsie!"

The girls both threw their arms around Elsie, then scampered away.

Elsie watched them and then retrieved her basket. When she got to the edge of the green, she could see Perkin's house.

To her surprise, there was a horse wagon in front. Servants were loading up trunks and baskets.

The family was going away. Perkin hadn't been lying about *that*.

So why make up a story about the plague? The family often traveled. Perkin was always bragging about their trips.

Why would he say they were fleeing the plague? Why lie about Princess Joan?

Because he's a bully, Elsie thought, *and he likes to make trouble*.

Elsie shook her head, knocking Perkin from her thoughts. Instead, she pictured the gleaming silver bowl studded with rubies.

She had more important things to worry about than Perkin and his lies.

CHAPTER 11

ABOUT TWO HOURS LATER

Elsie gripped her bow as she slowly made her way through the forest. She walked along the stream and climbed the big hill. She'd been on this path so many times in her life. But the forest seemed darker than usual.

With each step, her courage seemed to drain away, like water leaking from a cracked bucket. Every sound stopped her in her tracks — a snapping twig, rustling leaves.

At one point she was sure there was someone close by. She ducked between two trees, gripping her bow.

A squirrel skittered by. Elsie lowered her bow, shaking her head.

What was wrong with her?

All she had to do was find the chest, grab the bowl, and rush back home. And here she was, huddled in the trees, afraid of a squirrel!

She thought of Papa.

He was never scared, and he'd had to face thousands of fierce French knights!

She took a breath and pressed on, moving deeper into the forest. She climbed over the fallen oak and came to the grassy spot where she and Humphrey had seen the rabbit. She hadn't been paying attention as they'd chased it into the thicket of trees. But finally, after a few wrong turns, she found it.

Stepping inside the ring of tall bushes, she worried she wouldn't be able to find the place where the outlaws had hidden the chest. But then she spotted a tree stump that looked familiar. Nearby, there were boot prints in the mud. She followed them to a thick, tangled bush. She pulled aside some of the thorny brambles.

And there it was.

She pulled the chest out a few feet so she could open the lid. There were at least ten different gold and silver objects — bowls and cups, candlesticks, and crosses. Most were studded with bright flashing gems — red and blue, green and orange, yellow and pearly white.

Elsie couldn't begin to guess how much money all this was worth — maybe a king's fortune. Just one candlestick would fetch more money than most people in Brambly earned in their entire lives.

She found the church bowl. It was duller than she remembered, dented and scratched in spots. The rubies were very small. It was probably worth much less than the others.

But to Father William and the people of Brambly, it was priceless.

A thrill ran up Elsie's spine.

She'd done it!

But then her ears pricked — she heard footsteps, and this time she knew it wasn't the skittering paws of a squirrel or a rabbit.

It was the sound of someone running fast — and getting closer by the second.

Elsie tossed the bowl into a bush, closed the lid of the chest, and quickly shoved the chest back into its hiding place. A few paces away was a tree, rotted from the inside out. She managed to squeeze herself inside. Seconds later, someone burst through the trees.

It was Humphrey!

He must have been following her!

But before she could call out for him, she heard men's voices — shouts and curses.

Elsie's blood turned to ice. She recognized Grimwood's voice — and that dirty-bearded outlaw's, too.

She wanted to scream out to Humphrey. But what good would that do? The men would hear her — and capture them both. And Humphrey knew he was in danger. He was looking for a hiding place. But as he headed into the bushes, his tunic got caught on a thorny branch. He tried to tear himself away. He pulled at the fabric and twisted his body. But it was too late.

"Stop!" a voice boomed.

And there they were. Grimwood. Dirty Beard. Two other outlaws in their fancy, filthy clothes. Of course they saw Humphrey. Dirty Beard stormed over, grabbed Humphrey by the arm, and viciously yanked him out of the thorns.

He dragged him back to Grimwood.

Elsie stood there, frozen in fear. A wasp buzzed from somewhere close and then landed on her cheek. But she didn't dare move to brush it away. She watched in terror as Grimwood walked slowly up to Humphrey.

Grimwood's tiny black eyes glistened. They were like the eyes of a crow Elsie had seen pecking at the rotting flesh of a dead fox.

"What are you doing here?" Grimwood barked.

"I was just . . ." Humphrey's voice was shaking. "I was hunting for a rabbit."

"Where's your bow?" Dirty Beard demanded.

"Um, uhhhhh . . . I dropped it," Humphrey said.

"You know what happens to liars?" Grimwood asked Humphrey. "They have their tongues ripped out."

Elsie's heart was hammering so hard she thought her chest would explode.

"Get rid of him," Dirty Beard growled. "He's a nothing. Just another peasant runt. He won't be missed."

"Do it," Grimwood said. "Leave his body to the wolves."

The outlaw stepped forward, slowly pulling a dagger from his belt.

CHAPTER 12

Elsie had to save Humphrey. But there were five men with swords and daggers. She was one girl with a flimsy bow and four hand-carved arrows.

The wasp was now buzzing in her ear like it was trying to tell her something. It zoomed away, disappearing into the branches of a tree up ahead. And that's when she saw it — the wasp nest. It was right above Grimwood.

She remembered a story Papa had told her, about how soldiers defend a castle that's under attack. To stop enemy soldiers from climbing over the castle walls, the soldiers dump pots of boiling oil on the enemies' heads.

Elsie studied the wasp nest. It was gigantic, a light gray oval bigger than a horse's head. Inside there had to be ten thousand wasps. Maybe more.

Ten thousand wasps would be even better than boiling oil, she thought.

And before she even realized what she was doing, she'd slipped out of the tree. Barely breathing, she slid her bow off her shoulder and grabbed an arrow from her back.

She could practically hear the words of the archer commander calling to her.

Ready your bow!

Nock!

She loaded the arrow and pulled back on the string.

Aim!

She pointed the arrow at the top of the wasp nest.

Elsie took a deep breath.

"Humphrey!" she screamed.

The men whirled around.

"Run!" she shouted.

Humphrey scrambled to his feet and ran away.

Loose!

Elsie fired the arrow.

Feshoooooom!

She watched as it sped through the air, hitting a bullseye in the center of the wasp nest.

Thwack!

The arrow knocked the nest from the branch.

It hit the ground just inches from Grimwood's feet, splitting open.

Smoke seemed to gush out of a crack in the nest.

Except it wasn't smoke.

It was wasps, hundreds, then thousands, a massive swirling swarm of stinging creatures. Their furious buzz filled the air.

BZZZZZZZZZZZZZZZZZZZZZZZZZ!

"Look out!" a man screamed.

Elsie raced after Humphrey, who was waiting for her at the edge of the thicket. She looked

back and saw men falling to the ground, rolling and twisting and frantically waving their arms to escape the attacking wasps. Their bellowing cries and curses seemed to shake the trees.

Elsie and Humphrey clasped hands and raced away. They ignored the thorns that tore at their clothes and raked their flesh. They leapt over the giant fallen tree and splashed through the stream. They slid down the muddy hill.

They didn't slow down until they were back in Brambly.

CHAPTER 13

Elsie and Humphrey stopped at a small pond in the middle of a sheep meadow. They had to clean themselves up — they were both covered in mud and sweat.

A large flock of sheep grazed behind them, their *baaaa*'s filling the air. But all Elsie could hear was her own scolding voice inside her head.

Fool! Failure! Weakling!

Some warrior she was. She'd failed in her mission. She'd almost been caught. And because of her, Humphrey had almost been killed.

Elsie sat back in the grass and took a breath.

Neither of them had spoken during their frantic run out of the forest. And Humphrey looked the way she felt — stunned and scared. His hands shook as he tried to pick thorns from his tunic.

"I'm sorry, Humphrey," Elsie finally said.

"Why are you sorry?" he asked. "You saved my life!"

"But it's because of me that you were in the forest," Elsie said. "You were looking out for me and —"

"I didn't follow you!" Humphrey said. "I had no idea you would be there. I was going to get the bowl myself . . . to surprise you."

"What?!" Elsie cried.

"You promised Jonah you wouldn't try to get it back. *I* didn't promise him." He leaned toward her. "I knew how much you wanted it, Elsie."

"You went into the forest . . . by yourself . . . for me?" she said.

Humphrey nodded. Their eyes locked.

But then Humphrey looked away.

"What's going to happen now?" he asked.

"Grimwood saw us. Remember what Jonah said about him?"

How could Elsie forget?

Grimwood will destroy anyone who threatens him.

What would he do if he found them now?

He'd lock them both away — or worse. And if anyone in Brambly tried to stop him, he'd destroy the whole village. Like he had done to Westerly.

Elsie pictured everything in flames — their church, the houses, the market stalls.

Baaaa. Baaa. Baaa.

She looked at the big flock of sheep. There had to be fifty of them, and they all looked alike. If only she and Humphrey were sheep. They could blend into the flock, and Grimwood would never find them.

But wait . . .

Maybe, to Grimwood, they weren't so different from sheep.

"Humphrey," she said. "Remember how that outlaw said you were a nothing?"

Humphrey cringed. "Just another peasant

runt," he said, imitating the man's deep, rasping voice.

"But maybe it's good that they think of us that way," she said. "We're just like the hundreds of other peasant . . . runts . . . living on Lord Norling's lands. To Grimwood, we must all look the same. Like those sheep look the same to us."

Humphrey eyed the sheep, scrunching his brows together.

"Maybe that's true," he said finally. "And all he really cares about is his treasure, right?"

Elsie nodded. She felt her body relax. Maybe they really could put all this behind them.

"We can never tell anyone what happened," she said.

Humphrey nodded.

"It will be our secret," he said. "For life."

He spit into the palm of his hand. Elsie spit in hers, and they rubbed their slimy hands together. Now the promise was sealed.

She and Humphrey made their way across the meadow. But there was a bitter taste in her mouth, worse than any of Granny's broths.

It wasn't right that the church treasure was lost.

It wasn't right that Grimwood would get away with this.

It wasn't right that people had to live in fear.

But Elsie understood now.

She wasn't a warrior like Papa. She wasn't like the fierce knight in the old dragon story.

She was a girl. A peasant.

A nothing.

She and Humphrey were almost at Elsie's house when she remembered — Jonah! She'd promised Granny she'd invite him to supper. They hurried across the churchyard back to his house. The wagon was still out front. The horse, Kibby, neighed and snorted when he saw them. He was in the same spot as yesterday, which was strange. Jonah usually brought him around back to graze this time of day.

They knocked on the door, but there was no answer.

"Look!" Humphrey cried, pointing to a small black mound on the ground near the door.

Elsie's stomach flipped when she realized it was the black rat. It was dead, its small tongue hanging from its open jaw. Maggots squirmed all over it.

A feeling of dread came over Elsie.

She took a breath and opened the door.

CHAPTER 14

Elsie and Humphrey stepped inside. A ghastly stench practically punched them in the face. Elsie's hands flew up to her nose to try to block it, but it was no use. Willow the cat shot out the door and disappeared into the grass.

Elsie and Humphrey backed up out the door, coughing and gasping, sucking in clean, fresh air.

"Oh Lord!" Humphrey cried. "What could it be?"

The smell was sickly sweet, like rotting apples, but with something else . . . the putrid stench of the butcher shop on a hot day. Spoiled meat. Blood.

Elsie prayed Jonah wasn't here. But she knew in her heart he was. She wanted to bolt away. But Jonah was like family. They had to find out what had happened.

"Come on," she said, holding her arm over her nose and mouth. She took a last breath of clean air and stepped inside. The smell seemed to attack her, surrounding her like that swarm of wasps. Her nose burned. Her eyes watered. Humphrey was right behind her, his hands over his face.

The room was cold — there was no fire in the hearth. The water bucket was turned over. A chair lay on its side. And that smell . . .

Fear churned in the pit of Elsie's stomach as they stepped toward the sleeping room and eased open the door. The smell was even stronger. Elsie saw an empty straw mattress. She heard heavy breathing and low moans.

And there, on the floor, was Jonah. He was curled on his side, wearing only his leggings.

Elsie and Humphrey both flew over to him, ignoring the smell.

"Jonah," Elsie said, grabbing one of his hands. "What happened to you?"

His limp hand was scalding hot.

"Wa . . . ter," he groaned.

"I'll get some!" Humphrey said, jumping up and flying out the door.

Elsie clutched Jonah's hand in one of hers. His face was twisted, his eyes blinking madly. He seemed far away, trapped in a nightmare of fever and pain. It didn't seem possible! She thought back to yesterday. Yes, he was tired. But he'd been smiling, telling stories, hauling heavy piles of fabric.

A voice echoed through Elsie's mind. It was the voice of the traveler who had warned them of the new sickness.

It kills in hours.

They die in agony.

Jonah let out a cry. He pulled away from Elsie, his body twisting in pain. His arm flew up over his head.

Elsie stared in horror.

Under his arm was an enormous lump the size of an apple. The skin over it was furious red and cracked open like an egg. Yellow pus and blood leaked out.

The lump . . . a *bubo*.

A wave of terror crashed over Elsie.

That traveler hadn't been making up stories.

Perkin hadn't been lying.

This new sickness — the plague — it was real.

And it was here, in this room. Inside Jonah.

Humphrey stumbled in with a pitcher of water and a mug.

Elsie turned to him, her eyes filled with tears. "Get Granny!"

CHAPTER 15

Almost everyone in the village came to Jonah's funeral. A cold rain fell. Elsie stood between Humphrey and Granny, shivering. She was dizzy, and her eyes ached, probably from crying so much.

Humphrey let out a sob as four men carried Jonah's coffin and carefully lowered it into the grave. Elsie looked away. Shivering harder now, she pulled her damp cloak tighter. She didn't realize that sadness could make her so freezing cold. And thirsty. She wished she could drink up the rain that was falling.

It was raining so hard, like the sky was crying for Jonah. Elsie was crying, too. She knew how he had suffered. Granny had done all she could to help him. She'd cooled him down with wet rags. She'd spoken softly to him, her voice soothing and calm. If she'd been disgusted by the terrible smells, she never showed it.

Elsie and Humphrey had sat outside, praying for Jonah. But soon Granny appeared.

"Please go get Father William," she said quietly.

And that's when they knew that Jonah would die. Dying people needed to say a last confession before they passed. That way they would go right to heaven.

And now there was a giant hole in their small village. She eyed the people around her — men and women, little kids, people she'd known her whole life.

Who would be taken next?

Already five more people in the village had died. The wool seller and his wife. Peter the blacksmith and his wife, Anna — they were Abra and Lucy's parents. A farmer who'd recently returned from a trip to Melcombe. They'd all shared the high fever, the blinding headache, and the crushing body aches. The horrid buboes.

And now others were sick.

Elsie thought of Perkin's family, who were far from Brambly by now. Some said they were cowards, running away when people needed to stick together. But already two other families were making plans to leave.

And could anyone blame them? Wouldn't everyone flee if they had a horse and a wagon? Elsie guessed maybe they could take Jonah's. But Granny was the only healer in the village. She'd never leave people when they needed her most.

Also, there seemed to be no hiding from the plague. Nobody was safe — not even Princess Joan. It turned out that Perkin hadn't lied about her, either. She'd died in France, where her ship had stopped on the way to Spain.

· · ·

After Father William said the final prayers, they all made their way to the churchyard. The sun had come out, but Elsie was still freezing cold. Her teeth chattered. She was feeling more desperate for something to drink. Her muscles ached, probably from standing around for so long. All she wanted was to curl up on her mattress with Willow, Jonah's cat. She lived with Elsie and Granny now.

A small crowd surrounded Granny.

"Are you sure there is no cure for this plague?" Tilda, the baker's wife, was asking. She held her plump baby girl, Gertie, close.

"I wish there was," Granny said. "All we can do is make a person comfortable and try to cool the fever."

"What about bleeding?" asked Edward the butcher.

Bleeding — bloodletting — was the most common cure for fevers and other illnesses, especially at church hospitals. The monk would use a sharp blade to open a person's vein. Blood would pour out, filling a large bowl. They believed it cooled overheated blood.

Elsie shuddered. She'd never been bled — Granny didn't believe in it.

"Bleeding weakens the person," Granny said. "It makes them die more quickly."

"I want to know where this sickness came from," Robert the baker cried.

This was the question that had been swirling for days.

"Could it be some kind of curse?" asked Wanda the egg lady.

"Certainly not," Granny said. She didn't believe in magic and curses, though many did.

"What about the planets?" Oliver the fruit seller asked. "I hear Saturn is high in the sky, and it's well known that Saturn brings illness."

Each person in the crowd seemed to have a different idea.

The Widow Brewster thought it might be an earthquake somewhere far away.

"It opens the ground and lets poisonous air seep out," she said.

Tilda said it could be a punishment from the heavens, which Elsie knew wasn't true. Father William always said God loved them all. He didn't use sickness to punish people.

None of the ideas made any sense to Elsie. For some reason, Elsie kept picturing that black, hissing rat that had jumped out of Jonah's wagon. And the red fabric, crawling with fleas. But she wasn't thinking straight. How could she, with her head pounding and her teeth chattering?

She shivered harder and wobbled a little. Granny turned, looking at her worriedly.

"What is it, child?" she said. She put her hand on Elsie's cheek and Granny's eyes filled with fear.

"You're burning up! You're —"

But the sound of galloping horses cut Granny off. Four men on horseback stopped at the edge of the churchyard. Three were wearing white-and-yellow tunics — that meant they were Lord Norling's soldiers. The fourth man was dressed in black leather.

Elsie's guts turned to jelly. Humphrey gasped.

It was Grimwood.

CHAPTER 16

Hateful whispers about Grimwood rippled through the crowd.

"What is that devil doing here?"

"Brute!"

But everyone went silent as he got off his horse and strode into the crowd.

Granny had wrapped her arm around Elsie's shoulder. Humphrey inched over to them and huddled close.

He whispered into Elsie's ear.

"What should we do?"

His voice sounded strange, like he was calling to her from very far away. Elsie tried to answer, but her mouth wouldn't open.

She watched what was happening around her — Father William hurrying over to Grimwood, the men in white and yellow moving through the crowd. But everything looked blurry, like Elsie was underwater.

"What brings you here to Brambly, Sheriff?" Father William said in a polite but nervous voice.

"We are searching for two dangerous children," he said. "They attacked some of my men in the forest three days ago."

His words echoed painfully through Elsie's pounding skull.

Dangerous. Attacked.

"No children from Brambly would do such a thing, Sheriff," Father William said.

Grimwood ignored him.

"These children are working for a gang of outlaws," Grimwood went on. "They are stealing from churches throughout Lord Norling's lands."

Gasps rose from the crowd.

"The boy has brown hair," Grimwood said. "He wears a brown tunic and the girl . . . the girl carries a bow and wears a blue dress."

Blue dress. Blue dress. Blue dress.

With shaking hands, Elsie tried to pull her cloak more tightly around herself. But there was no point. Everyone in the village would know he was looking for her. Her dress made her stand out. Like a sheep with blue fur.

She waited for people to start shouting her name.

But the crowd stayed silent.

"Do not try to hide these children!" Grimwood bellowed. "I will make this whole village suffer for their crimes!"

He'd burn Brambly, like he did Westerly. Elsie didn't doubt it. She had to stop him!

Before she even knew what she was doing, Elsie had pulled herself free of Granny's grip.

She staggered over to Grimwood. A gust of wind blew open her cloak.

"You are a liar!" she screamed.

But her screams came out as rasps.

Her vision flickered. And before her eyes, Grimwood's body seemed to stretch and widen. Suddenly he was bigger than the church. His black tunic turned to green scales; his black eyes glowed red. Fire shot from his mouth.

She blinked, and the dragon disappeared. Grimwood was moving toward her, his eyes filled with hatred. She noticed red welts on his face — wasp stings.

He shouted to his men.

"Take her!"

Elsie turned to run. But her legs gave way, and she crumpled to the ground.

"Leave her alone!" Granny cried. "She's sick!"

Sick?

And that's when Elsie understood.

Grimwood had hunted her down. But another killer had found her first. It had been attacking her all day.

Not a dragon. Not an outlaw or an enemy knight.

The thirst. The shivering. The pounding ache.

Elsie had the plague.

Voices shouted all around her.

Rough hands grabbed her arms.

And then everything went dark.

CHAPTER 17

Elsie had never felt such pain before. Her entire body throbbed, from the top of her head to the tips of her toes. She was freezing cold — like she'd been plunged into an icy river. And then there was the thirst — the terrible, terrible thirst.

This plague had taken over her body. It was like an evil creature inside her. It was chewing apart her bones. Clawing her guts. Crushing her chest.

This plague was tearing her apart.

Soon there would be nothing left.

•   •   •

Elsie sat up in terror.

Where was she? What was this dark and freezing place?

And then she understood — she was in a dungeon!

Grimwood and his men must have brought her here. Or maybe Granny had done it after all — to punish Elsie for sneaking into the forest.

"I'm sorry!" Elsie screamed.

But nobody answered. She tried to get up, but something held her down. She must be chained to the wall!

And wait, what was that skittering sound, that hissing?

Rats! She could see their hideous shadows in the darkness. *Stay away! Stay away!*

But they were everywhere. And now they were crawling all over her, biting into her flesh.

No! No! NOOOOOOOOOOOOOOOOOO!

· · ·

Screeeeee! Screeeeee! Screeeeee!

What was that terrible noise?

It was all around Elsie.

She lay there, too terrified to breathe.

And then she saw it — two glowing red eyes right above her.

Fiery breath blasted down on her.

The dragon! It had come for her!

She turned, curled into a ball. But she felt its claws dig into her back.

It lifted her up into the air, flapping its hideous, leathery wings.

Let me go! Let me go!

.   .   .

Where was she now?

Why was she soaking wet?

She heard soft voices, felt someone gripping her hand.

She opened her eyes. Was that Granny?

No. There was a man next to her, speaking softly.

Father William.

This must be the end, Elsie thought.

I'm dying.

I'm dying.

CHAPTER 18

The next time Elsie opened her eyes, she wasn't in a dungeon. She saw no rats, no dragons.

Her body no longer hurt. She was not freezing or burning. Breathing deeply, she smelled roses and mint.

This must be heaven.

Or a dream?

She slowly sat up, blinking in the sunlight. Her mind cleared. And she saw that she was at home, on her mattress.

Very slowly, it all came back to her.

Jonah's funeral. Grimwood. The endless nightmares.

The sickness — the plague.

No, this was not a dream. She was awake.

She was alive.

Mrreowww! Mrreowww!

Elsie looked down. There was a white cat — Willow! The cat stepped onto the mattress and snuggled up close to Elsie, purring loudly.

"Granny?" Elsie called. But her voice was barely a whisper.

She lay there, listening. But she heard no sounds from the other room.

Dread gripped her heart.

What if Granny . . .

She forced herself to get up from her mattress. At first, her legs wouldn't hold her up. She steadied herself against the cold wall until some strength finally returned.

With shaky steps, she slowly made her way across the small sleeping room.

She paused before she opened the door.

She had no idea how long she'd been in that bed. Who else had gotten the plague? What had happened to Granny? What would she find on the other side of this door — and beyond?

What . . . and who . . . was left?

Mrreowww.

Willow had followed her to the door. She nudged Elsie's leg with her little nose.

Go on, she seemed to be saying.

After a few shaky breaths, Elsie opened the door. She stepped into the front room.

Granny wasn't there.

Elsie gripped a chair, afraid she'd fall.

She felt like she was lost in another fever nightmare. Except she had no doubt that this was real.

But then the front door opened. Elsie held her breath. And there she was — Granny. She stepped inside with the milk bucket.

She looked up and saw Elsie. Her entire face lit up. Tears welled in her bright blue eyes. She put the milk bucket on the floor. And then she practically flew across the room. She grabbed hold of Elsie and lifted her off the ground. It was a long time before they let each other go.

Granny helped Elsie to a chair and poured her a mug of milk.

"Drink slowly," Granny said.

Neither of them spoke as Elsie drank her milk. Granny poured some milk into a dish for Willow. They sat quietly for a long time.

But eventually, Granny began to share all that had happened over these past weeks.

"You were so very sick, child," Granny said, her eyes softening to sadness. "You were raving with nightmares. You kept trying to run outside."

The dungeon.

The dragon.

The rats.

Elsie shuddered.

Granny refilled Elsie's mug. Willow curled up on Elsie's lap.

"You finally started to get better three days ago," Granny said. "The fever went down and didn't come back. And that's when I knew you were going to make it through this. You came back to us," Granny said with a smile.

"What about Grimwood?" Elsie asked fearfully.

Granny's blue eyes narrowed. "That devil was ready to take you and Humphrey away," Granny said, her eyes blazing with anger. "But even he could see you were sick. And as soon as he heard the word *plague*, he and his men rode off as fast as they could."

Father William and the Widow Brewster helped Granny get Elsie back home.

Granny's eyes softened again, the anger turning to sadness.

"We've lost so many of our friends," she said.

More than forty people in the village had died.

Robert the baker and Tilda. Seth the tailor. Oliver the fruit man. Edward the butcher and his family . . .

"You are one of the only people with this plague who's gotten well, Elsie," Granny said. "And every day, more people become ill."

Elsie sat there, too stunned to speak. This was

worse than any nightmare or old legend. Even a dragon couldn't snatch forty people in three weeks.

Elsie's heart felt like it was crumbling apart. And there was still one person Granny hadn't mentioned.

"Granny," Elsie said softly. She swallowed hard, afraid to even say the words. "What about Humphrey?"

Granny shook her head.

"I don't know."

"What do you mean?" Elsie asked. "Did Humphrey . . . is he . . . ?" Elsie swallowed the lump in her throat. "Tell me the truth, Granny!"

"I'm telling you the truth," Granny promised. "Humphrey and his uncle disappeared after Jonah's funeral. Ralph has a cousin somewhere on the other side of the forest. They must have gone there."

"So he's safe?" Elsie begged. "Do you promise he's safe?"

Granny looked at Elsie. She reached over and took her hand.

"I hope so, Elsie," she said.

Elsie saw the doubt in Granny's eyes. Of course she couldn't make promises. The plague was everywhere.

Nobody was safe.

CHAPTER 19

For two more weeks, Elsie was so weak she stayed mostly in bed. Granny was gone much of the time, tending to the sick. Elsie was terrified that Granny would get the plague. But the days went by and Granny stayed well.

"Some people seem not to get sick," Granny told her. "I think they have some kind of natural protection."

Peter the blacksmith and his wife had died. But Abra and Lucy hadn't gotten sick at all. Father William had been by the bedside of everyone who had died. But like Granny, he'd stayed well.

Another week went by. And still Elsie was on her mattress most of the time. Willow didn't leave her side. Elsie would get up to eat and wash. But then she'd have to go back to sleep.

Meanwhile, Granny never seemed to rest. She cooked healing broths and hearty stews for Elsie. She tended to the sick. And she was spending hours each day at the church.

Father William had turned it into a home for children whose parents had the plague or had passed away. Abra and Lucy were both there. So was Tilda's baby girl, Gertie. The Widow Brewster and some other women were helping care for them all.

Slowly, Elsie's strength returned. And one afternoon, she decided it was time to go out. It was almost Christmas, and the village was covered with a dusting of snow. Elsie bundled up and stepped into the cold.

Walking across the village green, her shoes

crunched on the icy ground. An eerie quiet hung over the village. The tavern was closed — the owner and his family had died. The butcher shop was shuttered. The bakery, too. No smiling faces waved from doorways.

Elsie flashed back to the last time she was here, on market day. She remembered the stalls piled high with ripe apples and speckled pears. She could practically hear the echoes of happy voices and laughter.

That was just two months ago.

How was it possible that the world could change so quickly?

She walked past the shuttered windows and doorways to a row of small peasant houses. Three looked abandoned, including Humphrey's.

She walked up to the door and stood there. An arrow of pain shot through her chest.

"Where are you?" she called out.

Her voice echoed into the emptiness.

Elsie thought of all the time she'd spent complaining about everything that wasn't right.

She closed her eyes, picturing Humphrey's

goofy smile, hearing the sound of his voice.

She squeezed her eyes shut.

Why hadn't she ever taken even a minute to tell Humphrey how much he meant to her?

The weeks passed, and Granny kept asking Elsie to come to the church.

"Abra and Lucy are asking for you," she said.

Elsie wanted to see the little girls. But what could she do for them — or anyone?

The longer she stayed inside the house, the easier it was to pretend the plague had never come to Brambly. She didn't have to think about all the people who were lost. She could imagine that everything was like it was before.

"I'm still very tired," Elsie would fib. "Maybe tomorrow."

Then one afternoon while Granny was gone, Father William came to the house. At first Elsie felt worried — had something happened to Granny?

He smiled warmly at Elsie. "I need you — at the church."

Father William needed her?

Elsie opened her mouth to explain that she was still so tired. But she couldn't bring herself to lie to Father William. And how could she explain the real reason — that she was scared, weak, useless?

She stood there, feeling ashamed. Father William must be so disappointed in her.

But he didn't seem disappointed. His eyes were filled with kindness — and understanding.

Willow appeared. She came up next to Elsie and gave her a nudge.

"Come," Father William said, opening the door and waving for Elsie to follow.

It was cold outside, but the sky was bright blue. A few people were out. They waved at Elsie. As Elsie and Father William got closer to the church, Elsie heard a sweet sound echoing through the air. At first, she thought it was birds. But it was winter, and the songbirds wouldn't be back for months.

The sound got louder. Elsie realized, with shock, that it was the sound of laughter coming from inside the church.

Little girls giggling.

Elsie and Father William stepped inside. Abra,

Lucy, and three other children were sitting around the Widow Brewster. The room felt warm and cozy and smelled like fresh bread.

The children all turned to look at her.

"Elsie!" Abra and Lucy shrieked.

The little girls sprang up and raced over to her. They threw their arms around Elsie, squeezing her so hard it was difficult to breathe.

Elsie hoped they'd never let go.

Elsie spent every day after that at the church. She made up games to play with the children. She sang songs and told them stories. She made one up about two brave little girls who fought a dragon, who scared it away so it never came back.

When she got home each night, she was too tired to worry or even think. She'd fall into bed with Willow and drop right off to sleep.

By the beginning of February, the plague loosened its grip on Brambly. A whole week went by and nobody got sick. Another week passed. And another.

Granny and Elsie's hopes rose.

But then early one morning, she and Granny awoke to a frantic knock on their door.

No, Elsie thought with dread.

Someone needed Granny, she was sure. The plague must be back.

Granny wearily climbed off her mattress. She threw a blanket around her shoulders. Elsie heard the front door creak open. She braced herself for sobs, for the news that the plague had returned. That another person would soon be lost.

A moment later, Granny came back and stood in the doorway of their sleeping room.

Tears were streaming down her face. But she was smiling. What was happening?

Another person appeared next to Granny.

It was Humphrey.

CHAPTER 20

ABOUT 15 MONTHS LATER,
THE NEXT APRIL

It was a bright spring morning and Elsie and Humphrey hurried through the forest.

The birds were singing. Bright purple flowers waved in the soft breeze.

A deep voice called out behind them.

"Wait for me!"

A tall, bearded man limped up the hill.

Papa.

He smiled at them and waved the walking stick the Widow Brewster had made for him. He'd broken his leg in his last battle before he came home. Elsie flashed back to how he'd looked when he first got back — skeleton thin, hunched over like an old man.

He'd regained his strength and his jolly smile — Granny and Elsie made sure of that. But his days as a longbowman were over. He wasn't sorry. He'd had enough battles, he'd said. Enough blood. He didn't even want to tell stories about the war.

And he said even less about what he'd seen on his long journey home. He'd passed through empty villages. Fresh-dug graves were everywhere. Sobs echoed through the air. His leg ached with each step. But the worst part was the fear in his heart. Would Elsie and Granny still be alive?

"I've never been more scared," Papa had told Elsie. "And then I opened the door, and there you both were. I . . ."

Papa got too choked up to say any more about that. And he didn't have to. For the rest of Elsie's life, she'd cherish the memory of that moment when Papa appeared. Thin. Weak. Alive.

"Which way?" Papa asked, when he'd caught up with them.

"This way," Elsie said, pointing down to the stream.

Papa gave his walking stick a twirl and they started to move. Staring up at the towering trees, Elsie thought back to the last time she and Humphrey were here, when they came looking for a rabbit. When they were laughing and joking about baby dragons. When Elsie's biggest worry was Granny being mad at her.

If only they could go back to those carefree days before the plague!

Before.

Before.

The word rang through her mind. But she gave her head a little shake to clear it away. There was no going back to before, no point in wishing for it.

She looked at Papa and Humphrey. She pictured Granny, bustling around their house with Abra and Lucy. The girls lived with them now. Every night they said prayers for the girls' parents, for Jonah, for all the friends who'd been snatched away. Willow slept with Abra and Lucy now, snuggled between them on their mattress next to Elsie's.

They'd all made it through, together. And here they were. There was no use trying to find what had been lost.

Except maybe . . . one thing.

It had been Papa's idea that they try to find the church treasure — the silver bowl.

"There's the tree!" Humphrey said.

The fallen oak tree. It took a while to find the thicket. The thorny bushes were taller. The weeds were thicker. But otherwise, it looked the same.

Memories swirled through Elsie's mind.

Grimwood.

Dirty Beard.

The dagger.

"That's where I hid," Elsie told Papa, pointing to the hollow tree.

Of course she'd told him the whole story, and

Granny and Abra and Lucy, too. The girls loved hearing it. Now when they picked flowers, they didn't turn them into princess crowns. They pretended they were arrows, to protect them from outlaws and dragons.

"Where was the wasp nest?" Papa asked.

"Up there," Humphrey said, pointing to a high branch.

Papa glanced at Elsie, shaking his head, smiling proudly.

"And that's where the chest was," Humphrey said. "I remember that tree stump."

Elsie followed him through the overgrown brush, pushing aside branches until they reached the spot.

But the chest was gone.

Elsie's heart sank.

Probably the bowl was gone, too. Forever lost. Like so much else.

A familiar hopeless feeling rose up inside her.

It's not right. It's not . . .

But she fought those words back, like a longbowman shooting them away.

With narrowed eyes, she scanned around her,

remembering the bush where she'd hidden the bowl. She pushed apart the branches and peered down—nothing.

She dropped to her knees, pushing herself through the thorns. And that's when she saw it — a glint of silver peeping up from some tangled roots. Her heart pounded as she clawed them apart. She ignored the pain in her fingers as she worked the bowl free. She gripped it tight as she slid out of the darkness.

"You found it!" Humphrey cried.

He and Papa rushed over. They worked together to brush away the dirt and mud from the bowl. Papa rubbed it against his cloak.

They all gazed at the bowl in amazement. It had been lying in the dirt for more than a year. Rained on. Snowed on. Baked in the summer heat. There were a few small dents. The silver needed to be polished, and it was blackened in spots.

But how brightly those rubies shined— even now.

They sparkled like the church window when the sun shined through.

Like Abra and Lucy's laughter.

Like Humphrey's goofy smile.

Like Granny's blue eyes.

Like the feeling inside Elsie right now, when she thought of bringing the bowl back to Father William.

Elsie clutched the bowl tightly to her heart.

Papa put his arm around her, and Humphrey led the way out of the thicket.

The dark forest surrounded them. The tall trees towered into the sky.

But some rays of sun shined through, lighting up a path that led them toward home.

KEEP READING!

Turn the page to learn more.

A GRIM AND FRIGHTENING JOURNEY

Dear Readers,

Sometimes I wish I had a magical machine so I could actually propel myself back to the time and places I write about in this series.

I imagine strolling the deck of the *Titanic*, or exploring New York City before the Revolutionary War. I'd love to soar through the sky on the *Hindenburg* or wander the streets of ancient Pompeii.

But there is one place I would never want to go — Europe in the 1300s.

Even before the Black Death struck, life was, for most people, extremely difficult, and often brutal. The average person was very poor, never learned to read or write, and worked as a farmer on land they didn't own. They had few rights, and little hope for ever creating a better life, no matter how hard they worked.

There were, of course, no cameras back in the Middle Ages. And the artwork that survives from that time mostly focuses on wealthy people and royalty. These are some of the few surviving drawings that show peasants and other regular people.

And there were dangers everywhere. England and France had begun fighting in what would become known as the Hundred Years War. Outlaws roamed the dirt roads. In years when crops didn't grow well, people often starved to death.

But the biggest risk was disease or infection. People died of illnesses that are easily cured today, like a sore throat or ear infection. A simple cut or blister could get infected . . . with deadly results. Being a baby was especially dangerous; many didn't survive their first year of life. In fact, some families didn't even give their children names until they were two or three. Death from illness was a constant risk, whether you were a peasant girl like Elsie or the daughter of a king, like Princess Joan.

But even for people used to illness, the Black Death came as a ghastly, terrifying shock. The disease — known today as bubonic plague — was vicious. The sudden fever. The crushing aches. The terrible thirst. Let's not even think about those huge, swollen, seeping, stinking buboes!

Princess Joan was a daughter of King Edward and his wife, Philippa. King Edward wrote of her death in a letter, saying Joan has been "snatched from us, our dearest daughter, whom we loved best of all . . ."

Exactly how many people died is impossible to say for sure. In many areas, people weren't able to keep written records of exactly what happened.

And if there were records, many have been lost over the centuries.

There are few paintings from the years during the Black Death. But there are many works of art from the Middle Ages that focus on death. This image is part of a large painting from the 1500s called the Triumph of Death with the Dance of Death, *by the Italian artist Giacamo Borlone de Burchis.*

But most historians agree that tens of millions of people died. Great cities like Constantinople (today's Istanbul, Turkey) and Florence, Italy, lost more than half of their populations. Some farming villages in England and France and Germany lost even more — and were abandoned.

The few written accounts of this time are truly terrifying to read. They describe a sickness that spread like wildfire, graveyards overflowing, wails echoing through near-empty villages.

At times I wanted to call my editor, Katie, and tell her I'd made a huge mistake in choosing the topic. But then I'd think of all the kids who'd asked me to write about the Black Death. I'd received hundreds of emails and letters. One day, in a school parking lot, I was stopped by a fourth grader named Holden.

"Are you going to write about the Black Death?" he asked.

"Why do you think so many kids want to read about that?" I asked back.

"Because of Covid," he said, leading me toward his school. "I want to know what it was like to be in a pandemic all those years ago."

Of course, that made sense to me and explained all those emails and letters. Having lived through Covid, you have a connection to people who lived through the Black Death nearly seven hundred years ago. And as I plunged into researching this topic, it was fascinating to compare the two pandemics.

The Black Death was far deadlier than Covid. That's because when Covid struck, scientists from around the world mobilized to create vaccines and medicines.

Doctors, nurses, and other hospital workers risked their own health to save the very sick. We understood that diseases spread easily in crowds, so we could protect ourselves and others by wearing masks and staying home when we were sick. All these efforts likely prevented millions more Covid deaths.

But in Europe in the 1300s, people had none of this scientific knowledge. The best medical school,

During Covid, doctors, nurses, hospital workers, and first responders risked their own health to protect and save others.

in Oxford, England, taught ideas that were thousands of years old. There were no cures for the plague. And often, treatments made a patient sicker. Bloodletting (also known as bleeding) was the most common treatment for plague and other illnesses.

It wasn't until the 1800s that germ theory was

Many believed that fevers were caused by too much heat or poisons in the blood. Bloodletting — cutting open a vein and letting blood gush out — was believed to be an effective cure. (It absolutely was not!)

finally accepted around the world. This was the idea that diseases were spread by microscopic creatures — bacteria and viruses. With this new understanding, scientists began to invent vaccines and medicines. For the first time, some illnesses that were once deadly could be prevented or cured.

But there are some surprising similarities between Covid and the Black Death. Like with the Black Death, many people were slow to accept that Covid could spread around the world. Not everyone agreed on what treatments would work.

Even in our time of modern science, Covid has caused death and disruptions in almost every part of the world. More than seven million people have died.

Will I write an I Survived book about Covid?

Thousands of kids have asked me this. I have told them that I feel it's still too soon. But I do know that as the years go by, there will be many books about Covid. And writers of those future books will want to hear about your experiences.

So, take some time to write down your memories and reflections about Covid. Keep those writings in a special place. You may consider saving a mask or other artifacts from your Covid experience, too.

After all, history is not just facts and dates. It's the real stories of regular people — like you and me. Your memories could provide important lessons — and hope — for people of the future.

QUESTIONS AND ANSWERS ABOUT THE BLACK DEATH AND PANDEMICS

WHAT IS PLAGUE AND HOW IS IT SPREAD?

In the 1300s, nobody had any idea what caused plague and how it was spread. Many believed that it was caused by clouds of poisonous air, or the way the planets were arranged in the sky. Others blamed innocent people for causing plague.

It wasn't until the late 1800s that scientists discovered that plague is a disease caused by a bacterium — a germ. The germ is now known as *Yersinia pestis*. It commonly lives in wild rodents, including rats, squirrels, prairie dogs, and marmots. Plague makes these animals sick, but it usually doesn't kill them very quickly.

It is possible for a person to catch plague by touching an infected rodent. But it's much more common for humans to get plague from fleas.

These tiny creatures often live on rats and rodents, feeding on their blood. A rat might have as many as two hundred fleas living on it, gorging themselves on the rodent's plague-infected blood.

When that rodent dies, the plague-infected fleas hop off and go searching for a new source of food. Humans make excellent hosts for hungry fleas looking for fresh blood to drink.

When that flea bites into a human, it still has infected rodent blood in its belly. As it begins to feed, the flea vomits up some of this blood, sending it directly into the new bite.

WHAT HAPPENS TO A PERSON WHEN THEY GET PLAGUE?

Within a few days of becoming infected, a person will start to feel sick. Symptoms include a fever, chills, headache, and body aches. In the most common form of plague — bubonic plague — a person's lymph glands become very swollen. We all have many of these tiny glands in our body — under our arms, in our chest, in our neck, and at the very top of our legs.

When we are healthy, we can't feel these glands. When a person gets sick with an illness like a cold or flu, it's normal for these glands to

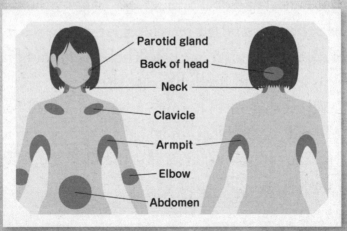

This diagram shows the locations of major lymph nodes in the upper body.

become a bit swollen. Then they go back to normal when the illness is over.

But when a person has bubonic plague, these glands can become grotesquely swollen. These are the lumps called buboes — and where the bubonic plague gets its name.

There are two other types — variants — of plague. *Pneumonic* plague also infects the lungs. *Septicemic* plague infects the blood. Though

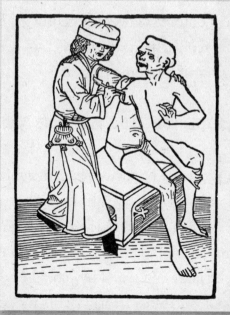

This is a woodcut from 1482, showing a plague doctor lancing a bubo hoping to cure someone of plague. This painful treatment was dangerous and did not help the sick person get better.

bubonic plague was most common during the Black Death, most scientists believe people were sickened by all three of the variants.

HAVE THERE BEEN OTHER PLAGUE PANDEMICS?

The bubonic plague has been sickening people for thousands of years. In the Bible, there are descriptions of an illness that could be plague. There have been many small outbreaks over the centuries. But there are three confirmed *pandemics* — worldwide outbreaks — of bubonic plague:

1. PLAGUE OF JUSTINIAN: 541–750

The first recorded pandemic began eight hundred years before the Black Death. In the years leading up to this outbreak, new trade routes had opened up. People from far-off lands could meet each other, traveling by land and sea. They could trade fabrics, spices, jewels, and other treasures. But they could also accidentally cause the spread of diseases like plague.

Beginning in Egypt, plague spread quickly

The Justinian plague outbreak is named after the emperor Justinian. He ruled a vast kingdom known as the Byzantine Empire. This empire fell in the 1400s, when its capital, Constantinople, was invaded by the Ottoman Turks. Today, this area is divided into separate countries including Turkey, Greece, Italy, much of northern Africa, and the Middle East.

throughout the Middle East and areas around the Mediterranean Sea. Plague made its way into Europe as well.

The city of Constantinople (which today we know as Istanbul, Turkey) was especially hard hit. Smaller outbreaks continued for more than 150 years until the disease finally faded.

Deaths: estimated tens of millions

2. THE BLACK DEATH: 1340s-1353

Scientists continue to debate when the Black Death in Europe actually began. Most agree that plague had been killing people throughout Asia and the Middle East in the years before the dates above. Very likely, traders and rats spread it along trading roads and sea routes between Asia and Europe. The first big outbreaks in Europe were in Italy, in 1347.

By 1353, it had sickened people in almost every corner of Europe, as well as Scandinavia and parts of Russia.

Deaths: estimated between 50 million and 200 million.

3. THE THIRD PLAGUE PANDEMIC

The last pandemic of the plague began in the middle of the nineteenth century in Yunnan, China. Like the other two, it quickly spread. India and China were hardest hit.

Chinese workers wearing protective clothing during the third plague pandemic.

It was during this pandemic that two scientists, using new and more powerful microscopes, were able to identify the bacterium — the germ — that caused plague. Kitasato Shibasaburo of Japan and Alexandre Yersin discovered the bacteria around the same time.

Due to some confusion over Shibasaburo's discovery, the germ was named for Yersin (*Yersinia pestis*).

Deaths: estimated 15 million

WHEN DID PLAGUE DOCTORS WEAR BEAKED MASKS?

In 1665, there was a major outbreak of plague in London. It was during this time that doctors began wearing special masks believed to protect from plague. Glass goggles were designed to protect the eyes. The beak was filled with fifty-five different herbs believed to protect against infection.

Unfortunately, this dramatic costume did not

stop the plague. In the end, between 75,000 and 100,000 people died.

Today, the beaked mask survives as a symbol of plague. It has even become a popular Halloween costume.

WHERE DOES THE TERM *BLACK DEATH* COME FROM?

This term was not commonly used until the 1800s. People who lived through the terrible time called the disease *the pestilence* or *plague*. In Italy, it was called *moria grandissima*, which means "the big death."

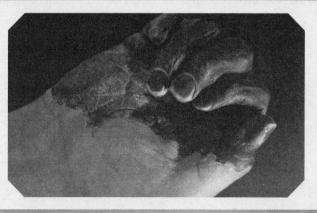

In the septicemic form of plague, an infected person's skin sometimes turns black, which may be why people came to call plague the "Black Death."

It's possible that the term *black death* refers to the blackening of the skin that happens when people get sick with the septicemic form of plague.

DO PEOPLE STILL GET PLAGUE?

Yes. Every year, between 1,000 and 3,000 people are diagnosed with plague around the world. It is most common in Peru, the Central African Republic, and the African island of Madagascar.

In the United States, about ten people are sickened by plague each year. Most cases happen on the West Coast, in the Rocky Mountains, and in the Southwest.

But luckily, plague is not the deadly disease it was in the past. Several modern medicines — antibiotics — work very well against plague. What's important is that the person gets to a doctor quickly. Because, left untreated, plague can still be deadly.

TO CONTINUE YOUR
READING JOURNEY

If you enjoyed this book, try reading one of the books below. They all feature characters who live in a similar time or face similar obstacles as Elsie and Humphrey.

Crispin: The Cross of Lead, by Avi, Scholastic, 2001
This amazing novel (one of my favorites) brings to life England in the years after the Black Death.

Fever 1793, by Laurie Halse Anderson, Simon and Schuster, 2002

This is another incredible novel, about a different deadly illness: yellow fever. A terrible outbreak happened in Philadelphia in the years after the American Revolution.

A Company of Fools, by Deborah Ellis, Fitzhenry and Whiteside, 2007

I loved this book about two very different boys who become friends as plague closes in on Paris, France.

SELECTED BIBLIOGRAPHY

I read many books and articles while researching my I Survived books. Here are the books that provided me with the most information on the Black Death.

The Black Death, by John Hatcher, Da Capo Press, 2008

The Black Death and the Transformation of the West, by David Herlihy, Harvard University Press, 1997

The Great Mortality: An Intimate History of the Black Death, by John Kelly, Harper Perennial, 2006

A Distant Mirror, by Barbara W. Tuchman, Alfred A. Knopf, 1978

A World Lit Only by Fire, by William Manchester, Little Brown, 1993

In the Wake of the Plague, by Norman F. Cantor, Free Press, 2001

The author in the medieval city of Santiago de Compostela, Spain. This area was one of the early hot spots of the Black Death pandemic.

Lauren Tarshis's *New York Times* bestselling I Survived series tells stories of young people and their resilience and strength in the midst of unimaginable disasters and times of turmoil. Lauren has brought her signature warmth, integrity, and exhaustive research to topics such as the September 11 attacks, the American Revolution, Hurricane Katrina, the bombing of Pearl Harbor, and other world events. Lauren lives in Connecticut with her family, and can be found online at laurentarshis.com.